Julius and Macy

A Very Brave Night

Annelouise Mahoney

two lions

To Makayla and Sienna, you are my favorite adventure.
And to Michael, who is never afraid of the dark,
thank you for walking beside me.

Published by Two Lions, New York
www.apub.com

Amazon, the Amazon logo, and Two Lions are trademarks of
Amazon.com, Inc., or its affiliates.

ISBN-13: 9781542007160
ISBN-10: 154200716X

The illustrations were created in watercolor.
Book design by Tanya Ross-Hughes

Printed in China
First Edition
10 9 8 7 6 5 4 3 2 1

There is a special place
Julius and Macy like to play . . .

. . . where they can be
anything at all.

"I'm the defender of
the forest," said Julius,
who loved being brave.

Macy was brave, too, in her own way.

Most nights Julius and Macy
liked to play heroes,
and tonight was no different.

"We'll capture something big," said Julius.

"Or set something free,"
said Macy.

It seemed as though they could play all night,
but even heroes need a snack sometimes.

They were sure they'd
packed cookies and nuts,
but their snacks were missing.

"The Night Goblin must have taken them!" said Julius.

"What's a Night Goblin?" asked Macy.

"He lives deep in the woods and
is taller than trees. He has
big yellow eyes and crooked teeth.
He's the worst kind of scary,"
said Julius.

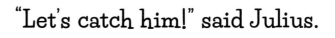

"Let's catch him!" said Julius.

"We need to be careful," said Macy.

They wandered deep in the forest
to a place they had never been before.

Then they heard it, a sound so terrible
it made them tremble.

Crunch
crunch
crunch!

"The Night Goblin!"
whispered Macy.

"It's REALLY dark in there,"
said Julius.

"Did you hear that?"
asked Macy.

"He sounds hungry," said Julius as they crept deeper into the cave.

"He could be around any corner," said Macy.

Crunch crunch crunch!

"The worst kind of scary," whispered Julius.

"What do we do?"
asked Macy.

"We stay brave,"
said Julius.

Then as if from nowhere,
they heard . . .

. . . a small
sigh
and a tiny
a-achoo.

Quietly, they stepped around the corner,
and there they found the Night Goblin.

"Julius," said Macy, "he looks kind of lonely."
She whispered an idea to Julius,
but he wasn't so sure.

But sometimes
being brave isn't about
being a superhero.

"Hello,"
Julius and Macy said together.

It turned out the Night Goblin wasn't even a monster at all.
His name was Sherwin, and he lived alone.

"I'm sorry I took your snacks," he said.
And he meant it.

When it was time to go home,
Julius and Macy wished their
adventure didn't have to end.

"Do you want to play with us?"
they asked Sherwin.

He did.

Even though he wasn't really sure how.

So Julius and Macy led the way.
And they only paused once,
because even heroes get
hungry sometimes.

And on this night, everything tasted especially delicious.